It's Time)

Rise Above

Now

GOOD IS NOT ENOUGH WHEN BETTER IS
AVAILABLE!

Shawn Johnson

It's Time You Rise Above, Now!

Rise Above Now

All scripture quotations are from the KING JAMES VERSION; our directional pathway is to live life more abundantly through the word of the HOLY BIBLE.

Copyright by: Library of Congress 2013

ISBN: 0-9787162-6-4

Cover Design: Parice Parker

Author: Shawn Johnson

F. O. L. P. H. Chief Editor's Team

Fountain of Life Publisher's House

Printed in the United States of America

It's Time You Rise Above, Now!

Rise Above Now

Fountain of Life Publishers House

P. O. Box 922612 Norcross G. A. 30010

**Phone: 404.936.3989 Please Send Manuscripts to Email:
publish@pariceparker.biz**

For book orders or wholesale distribution

email: sales@pariceparker.biz

Website: www.pariceparker.biz

It's Time You Rise Above, Now!

Rise Above Now

Shawn Johnson

It's Time You Rise Above, Now!

Rise Above Now

What inspired me to write this book? I have learned with God all things are possible. He placed a desire in my heart to share my story with the world and to be a voice that would cry out loud and tell His children that He wants the best for them and if they would be obedient then there would be no good things He would withhold from them. Everyone has a story to tell. What makes my story different from yours is not much. Your story has pain, my story has pain. Your story means everything to you and my story means just as much to me. It's just that I choose to put mine on paper. I have to be a light that will shine in darkness, after dealing with so many of life issues on a personal level such as low self esteem, anger, rejection, abandonment, feelings of inferiority, abortion, abuse both physical and emotional, divorce, sickness in my body, single parenting and

It's Time You Rise Above, Now!

so much more. I decided that I had to rise above these issues once I discovered who I am.

Shawn Johnson

Rise Above Now

Introduction:

I chose to use my life experiences as stepping stones to get me to where God would have me to be. All the hurts, suffering, and pain were used to birth me into my purpose to do the will of God. To tell someone that God can and will give you beauty from ashes. My mess was my test and my test became my message and my message gives an opportunity to help others to know they too can overcome all adversity in life.

I woke up one day and I decided that through God's word that I could have life and have it more abundantly. And when those words resonated in my spirit, I decided I only wanted God's best for my life. I no longer wanted to settle for less than what life had to offer. There is nothing cute about living beneath your means. Time out for good

It's Time You Rise Above, Now!

when better is available. Life does not have to be a death sentence nor does it have to end when we go through trials and struggles. My heart's desire is for you to discover who you really are and learn your worth in life and never settle for less than what God has for you, you were created to be more than a conqueror; you are an over-comer, you can, you will, and you shall rise above it all.

Shawn Johnson

It's Time You Rise Above, Now!

Rise Above Now

I chose GREATER and no more settling for less than God's best. In all areas of my life, healthy relationships are at the top of the list. Healthy relationships with my children, family, friends, co-workers, and all who cross my path.

Shawn Johnson

Chapter One

Seasonal Changes

In life we learn that people are in our lives for a season, a reason, and a life time. When we are born we do not get to pick our parents. Life chooses them for us. So if you're fortunate enough to be born with a silver spoon in your mouth and your family is what we say is functional, then count your blessings. My journey did not take that path as far as I am consciously aware of. As I reflect, I cannot remember my first five years on earth, not a glimpse. I cannot recall my earlier years of life. It's as if I woke up and realized life for me began when I was given to a family in Washington DC. The Thompsons were the first people I knew to shape my world. They were a

It's Time You Rise Above, Now!

loving husband and wife team and became their responsibility. I was an only child and I remember their love towards me and their strong parenting. I saw nothing negative being a child. So I can remember my days of mischievous acts of wrong doings because children will do devilish things. One incident I can recall was when I got in trouble for asking an adult for something my father said I could not have and it got back to my dad. Well because of my action I was sent to bed that night without dinner, which was punishment number one and punishment number two was a whipping. The waiting process to find out my punishment was in hope that my imaginary friend would keep me company. So I got to be alone for my actions. I remember spending many lonely days during those times for being bad. Especially when it came to schooling, I was not a bright child and I was a slow learner. My bringing home bad grades kept me in my room. Another thing that stood out I remember was being spoiled. I had everything I needed and most everything I wanted. I never *understood as a child why they celebrated my birthday on a day other than was on my birth certificate. My birthday was celebrated in October and not in November and I can remember thinking this is not the day I was born. That bothered me greatly because it made me wonder why this was the case. But for the most part, this would be the most functional environment I would experience as a child. During my stay I would no longer be the only child because the Thompsons received another gift from God when they were finally able to conceive a child of their own and I now had a little brother. I can remember spending summers in the country with my grandmother, but during one visit we went down south for summer vacation. Needless to say, this was the trip that I would not return to DC. During the summer trip to SC that year was the year I would be reunited with my birth mother. What started out as a visit to say hello to my mother ended with my staying in S.C. As my mother had received a call informing her that her father had just been killed, the Thompsons*

It's Time You Rise Above, Now!

asked me if I wanted to stay with my mother and I thought that I should. She was in a bad place at that time, and seeing me return was what she needed to heal. I was thrust into a lifestyle of dysfunctional behavior. My mother was young and single with two children younger than me, and I had to step in and become a helper to my family doing things that my mother did not do to care and provide for the family as a whole. When my mother and father were married she was only 16. Her first son was born shortly after wards, then came another son and a daughter with my father. I was the youngest of the three. She experienced a lot of abuse from her marriage. She said we never lacked for anything and had the best, but she could not deal with his abusive behavior, and alcohol and drug use. So she left everything behind to gain a peace of mind. She was not in a position to provide for her three children. So she gave up her parenting rights to my brothers because they were legally adopted, but I was not. She had too much responsibility before she was ready and she knew

It's Time You Rise Above, Now!

she was not in a position to be a good provider so she did the next best thing which was to place her children in the care of someone else.

Upon my return, I was forced to step up and do things before I was mature enough to handle the responsibility. I can remember standing in a chair over the stove cooking to feed my siblings, because mom was not around. So as I stood in the gap and fended for my siblings and myself, I encountered some unusual situations for a child, and because of the situations, I started to develop some bad feelings. Like why was I given away and why when I returned to my mother did she have two other children? I felt rejection early in life. I would ponder within why she would want me back. Was it for convenience to become her salve or was it because the taxpayer sent a check each month in care of Shawn to my mom? Bitterness and resentment set in my heart and I had something to prove as my rebellious nature grew. I set in my heart to not be like my mom, I will not turn out to be like her. I learned that my father died at the age of 30 from a heart attack. My mother and father were married and I had two older brothers but they were also gone and never returned until late in their adulthood. I was told that their adoption went through, that they were raised by a good family, and they would never lack for anything in life. So bitterness and rejection ran through my veins as a child. I felt as if life had cheated me and that my life was cursed. We struggled in those days not knowing where the next anything was coming from. I cannot remember when my mother worked a real job? She was not a high school graduate but still jobs was available. This was something I held against her. She lived below her means and I despised her actions. She also dealt with a lot of sickness in her life. She had tumors in her ear that gave her severe headaches that would put her down for days at a time. Another thing was she could never attain successful relationships with the men in her life. They came for a little while but all they left behind was heartache, disappointment and another sibling. I could not understand her life through my eyes. I did not like the living conditions we were subjected to and that my mother was so young and did a lot of foolish things. Though it is not right for me to judge her, as a child I could not understand why she kept looking for love in all the wrong places only to be left with three more children to feed on her own. No man was ever held accountable for their actions. As I share my story, believe me, I would get my chance to walk in her shoes. Here is a nugget: Because I was not mature and did not have the understanding, I held a lot of things against her. My love towards her was conditional because I never knew true love. My love towards my mother was superficial. I would come to a place in life that I would learn to forgive and love my mother unconditionally so I could learn to heal myself.

The dysfunction came when there was no food in the house for the family to eat and the utilities were being turned off for months at a time. I remember growing up and not even having a phone in the house. We always had to walk around the corner to use the pay phone. I remember living in trailer homes but I can say I never experienced living in the projects. We were one step from there however. Life did not spare me from being sexually mistreated as a child. One of the most painful things I had to do in my adult life was to confront my mother about an incident she allowed to happen to me by someone she knew, who sexually molested me . He would try to come around on several occasions when my mother was not home and out of fear I would not open the door. That experience left me with the impression that what happened to me didn't matter and that I was not important. I had little to no self worth, low self esteem and a sense of hopelessness. My childhood shaped and molded me for the relationships that I allow in my adult life.

If you are reading this book, it is because somewhere in your life you can relate. I had to take a serious look at my life. I did not like where I was going and I had the relationships to prove it. See, after one experience goes bad or wrong for so long, it comes a time when you get tired of being sick and tired. And with the series of bad relationships I had been in, it came a time for me to do something about them. I wanted better for myself. A mentor of mine said it best "Good is not good enough if better is available." It took me a long time to comprehend this but when I got it, it was life changing for me. I can hear Steve Harvey say "it's a shame when you're young and you make foolish choices that you have to pay for that experience when older."

There are several areas of focus in developing healthy relationships that I will address. I can say I did not read them in a book but as a result of what I experienced in the school of hard knots. My first unhealthy relationship began with myself. You can recall me saying I had no self worth, low self esteem and I dealt with hopelessness. I did not like myself at all. I walked around with a big sign around my neck and it read REJECT. Rejection became my biggest obstacle. I was so wounded and hurt from anger and bitterness that I wondered to myself if this was all life had to offer me. It was not a literal sign but it became something I internalized. That is how I saw myself for a long time. So many negative people would make me view myself in this light. The first rejection I felt was from my mother. How could she give me away and then have more children? That put me in a bad place for years even into my adulthood. The second rejection was from the school teacher/system. When I was growing up I was overweight and my mom used to buy all my clothes with the HUSKY tag on them so that was a strike against me. I had a poor self image of myself and because I am dyslexic, I had a hard time keeping up in school. Back then this term was not used so they would say, "she's slow, let's keep her back". The third rejection would follow me through my adult life with my career and personal relationships. These rejections taught me some valuable lessons. When *people could not understand me and they felt threatened many rejected me. They saw something in me that I did not see in myself. Case and point, I was being overlooked for advancement in the workplace and I was constantly involved in romantic relationships that did not last. I gave of myself freely, which allowed people to take advantage of me. I wanted to be accepted by people. I did not like being on the losing end. I tolerated people who mistreated me because I did not rejection. So people got away with doing things to me that they thought in their own eyes were right.*

I was so ready for change. I wanted so much more out of life and I was going to get it, starting with myself. And what better way to do this than to go back to the one who created me. Yes, I 'm talking about God. He created each and every one of us. Hear a nugget: Everything begins and ends with God. He is the alpha and omega. If I wanted to start to work on me I had to connect to Him. I'm not talking about the church. No! I'm talking about having a personal relationship with Him. One on one, the creator and me, the father and I, we were going to change my life for the better. Please note this process would not be easy but it was doable. No overnight changes but a life journey.

I had to change a lot of my way of thinking about myself. I had to allow God's spirit to come into my life and transform my mind. What was working against me was me believing in myself. It's one thing to believe in God but it is another thing to believe in God and myself. I fell short when it came to believing in me but God built my confidence. So if you ever decide you want more or better for your life, you must first start with the one who created you in His image. So I have to believe in myself; there is no way around it. I can hear my high school algebra teacher, Mrs. Myers, saying "Why go around Robinson's barn just to get to the front door?" What she was saying was why keep making the same mistakes when you can get the right answer the first time? Follow my leads and I assure you, you will start to have healthy relationships.

It was easy for me to form a relationship with God. I did not grow up in the church so my outlook was not tainted by religion. My relationship with God began when I was young. I always sensed His presence around me. I have this habit where I always talk to myself. You can call me weird but it was my defense mechanism which allowed me to stay sane in my own eyes. So I would hold conversations with myself to guide my choices and decisions in my life. All the conversations were not positive. Remember, my thought patterns were negative towards myself. Remember, I wore a sign around my neck that said "REJECT". And that is how I draw to myself lots of unhealthy relationships. I knew that God was working in my life at an early age. He was ordering my steps to guide me to a place where I would grow to truly have to lean and depend on him alone. Because I viewed myself a certain way, I never believed that college was in my future so one thing I asked God for was to let me travel and see the world and He answered my prayers. Though it came with challenge and hard work, I set out to join the United States Army after graduating from high school. During my high school years one of my greatest strengths was developing a great work ethic and I always faithfully showed up to tackle the tasks at hand. My mindset is to always "Make it happen," I have been working since the age of sixteen and I have yet to stop. There has never been a lazy bone in my body. Those habits guided me to want to join the military. So because I knew my weakness I set up a plan to get me to where I wanted to go in life. I was an average student in school, nothing more than a "C" throughout my entire school years, just enough to get by. I knew I was not college material so I had to do what it took to be good enough to get into the military so I purchased the ASVAB study guide during the summer of my junior year and I studied every chance I could get. It then came the time to take the test and I can today praise God because as a female I scored very well. My recruiters were amazed at my test results. I had scored especially high on the mathematics portion of the test. Now that the testing portion was behind me, my next challenge was to meet the physical requirements to enlist. And what a challenge it was. I can hear the phrase how bad do you want it?, Remember, I shared that I was a heavy child growing up. My weight had to be 128 lbs. to join the military for my height. Would you believe that? WOW! How could this be? How was I going to get that small? I began my journey to lose weight and Lord knows it was not easy. I love to eat; food gave me comfort due to my low self esteem issues. So I had to change my entire way of eating and I had to start working out. Suddenly I was on my way. The weight started coming off easily in the beginning but as I continued through the process, it started to slow to a minimum. When the weight was no longer coming off, I felt that I had hit a plateau. God was dealing with me as I was going through the process. I can recall going to weigh in twice and being denied entry because of my weight, 136 lbs then 131lbs. Okay I can hear the people at the MAPP station saying we'll see you in four months then two months because they only allow you to lose two pounds a month, that was the process, so home I go disappointed in myself and feeling really bad because I was in control and I just wanted out, away from my environment.

Another unhealthy relationship I had was with my mother. I held so many things against her. How she chose to live her life was a problem for me. Through her struggles and hardships I was taught what not to do and that I wanted a better life for myself. I did not want to be a single parent raising children I could not afford and choosing the wrong people to share my life with. I held her accountable for all her actions and that was not my place to do. I never felt I had my mother's love growing up. I was the child she gave away and the rejection I felt *from being unwanted left me bruised badly. And to think she had more children after giving me away was hard to swallow. I lived on the mindset that all I knew was all I needed. I would pay for that mindset because God was going to show me what unconditional love meant. I held myself captive for so long that I too was judged for my actions and some of the mistakes I made. I too walked in disobedience and I wanted God's forgiveness for myself. But before I could be forgiven I would have to learn to forgive my mother and all came through the process of time. The relationship between us was estranged for years. I left home at 16 years old. I had nowhere to go but I do remember working in downtown Charleston at the local Piggly Wiggly. One of my co-workers had an apartment and I camped out with her for a while during the summer until it was time to return to school. I lived in the North area and I still had a year of high school to complete. But there is always redemption in God. I learned to forgive my mother and today we have a good healthy relationship between us. We both are going through the healing process.*

My first unhealthy relationship with my boyfriend began. We dated in high school for two years. I went to his prom with him and things seemed good for a season, and then I discovered that there was another girl in his life and through their relationship a child had been born. He was in denial. He too was estranged from his own mother and through that time in my life I was lost. No one was in my corner, no one believed in me. I had no one to assure me that life was going to be alright for me, no one. I had nowhere to live. I tried reaching back to the family in DC but I was unable to make the connection. So one day I was walking and a lady pulled up beside me and asked if I needed a ride. I knew her but had never held a conversation with her. She was my boyfriend's mother and we talked awhile and I shared my story with her. She was a nice woman, not like the picture he had painted her to be. She offered to help me. She invited me to stay in her home with her and to give me a new beginning while continuing with high school. She became my mentor. She had helped develop my self- worth and caused me to dream and instill some discipline that I still needed in my life. The relationship between us was a win -win. She had someone to nurture and groom her when her own sons rejected her and I had someone to mother me because I need that in my life. But that caused my boyfriend to see me as the enemy now, which was okay because I wanted more for my life. During this season of my life I was moving forward. I was working at a clothing store and I was selected as a debutante for AKA and that helped mold me into a young lady wanting a life for herself. My relationship with my mother had ended and we were both so hurt that there was no communication between us for almost a year. I wanted better and I could handle the two worlds. So I shut the door on that part of my life for a very long time. I needed time to heal.

It's Time You Rise Above, Now!

I was determined to have a new direction for my life and I was not going to let anything stop me. During this season I became the mediator between my boyfriend and his mother. I was able to keep peace between them because he still wanted to be a part of my life because his life wasn't going anywhere. So he did everything in his power to help me to move forward with losing the weight. He was by my side throughout the whole process, and I was able to join the United States Army at 125 lb. I was moving onto the next chapter in my life but I now had a date January 25, 1988 which was the date to go to basic training.

And I decided on what field I wanted to be trained in and to gain experience in the military. I can still see the woman at the MAPP station helping me to decide on my Military Occupational Skill. A female recruiter encouraged me to choose electronic technician as my career. I viewed the slide and agree that I would become an electronic technician. During basic training I remember having my boyfriend and his mother visit me. So during this time my boyfriend and I got together. I felt ashamed because this was the day that he gave me crabs. Our entire barrack had to be disinfected and all the linens removed. This was so embarrassing for me but no one knew who had caused it. But I did ask myself how could I let this guy do this to me? Not only was it over but I never looked back at him ever again. I had put up more than my share of mistreatment from him. Talk about unhealthy relationships, I moved on and graduated from basic training. I now had 30 days of leave to use but I chose to move on to my AIT which lasted almost an entire year. See there was no one and I mean NO ONE I wanted to see back at home. I had my whole life ahead of me and I did not want to look back. After AIT which was a challenge for me, I made it and I was on my way to my first duty assignment. I was going to Germany for two years. While in Germany I connected with friends who were in AIT with me and my first year in Germany was interesting. I met new friends as well. I was learning the ins and outs of active duty, learning my new surroundings and customs, learning how to drive an autobahn and get my driver's license.

So for the first time I did not have to deal with any unhealthy relationships but the next one that would come into my life would shake my world. I was now twenty years old and mainly alone. Although people were around me, by now I was getting lonely and there were no suitable prospects to date. No one was approaching me. I met this male through my roommate and a year later he would become my first born child's father. I have learned that it's the storms of life that will draw us closer to God. I was in a bad place, so when the opportunity came for me to go and hear the word of God, I was there in church on base in Germany. This brought me so much strength and comfort that I thought I could handle my situation. How did I get here with another unhealthy relationship and with a man 10 years older than I? He was an *officer and his character was not one of his strong attributes. We were not in a relationship we just had relations and he was not interested in covering me. No, let me take ownership here. I let myself get pregnant and I was in no emotional position to terminate this pregnancy. I wanted this child in my life and at least I was working and I could afford to care for this child. When I was sixteen I had gotten pregnant and needed my mother to sign for me to terminate my pregnancy. I had vowed to myself never to have a child I could not take care of, and besides that, my experience weighed on me heavily. I had serious regrets for my actions but I stood strong in my conviction. And I was not at a place I wanted to deal with the emotion of my actions. So I set out to become a mother, and a good one I would be. I became determined not to raise my child the way I was raised. My relationship was one of physical, emotional and mental abuse. I was always being accused of cheating on him. He managed to say any negative word that would tear down my spirit and my self* esteem. I worked hard to stop myself from thinking negatively about myself and no man was going to put me in this place. It was so bad that I decided to leave Germany and go to WAR. My next assignment would be Fort Stewart, Georgia, and if that would give me the peace I needed to escape his grip over me then I would go. I was strong minded and independent and my son's father wanted to control my life. Where I went, who I socialized with, when I came and when I went. And any time he received my cookies, he managed to tear me down afterward. This was abuse and I could not take it anymore. There had to be more to life than this. I was too strong of an individual for him to control and he knew it. He wanted to keep me down so I would not leave him. When a person is always accusing you of doing something, you should take a closer look. They are trying to deceive you because they are trying to hide their flaws or shortcomings from you. I learned this early in life and because I had a child with this man I needed to be wise and stay one step ahead of *him. I had to ease my hand out of this lion's mouth and not get bitten. So I requested a change of duty station for myself. I let him believe everything was still good between us and I was going to just accept the abuse. But little did he know I had a plan; a plan to escape from him. I had to leave Germany and I wanted to take my son, so I learned the art of war. When the day came and I weathered the storm, I was released from the enemy stronghold over my life for a season. I'm leaving Germany and my son is in my arms and we were heading to my hometown of Charleston SC. While flying into the airport I had no plan in hand, just walking in faith. I had thirty days of leave to come up with a place for my son to stay when I left for Georgia. I agree with his father that he could come get him his son once he too returns state side. He had two month until he would become discharge. So after getting off the plane I call my ex-boyfriend's mother and when she answered I told her I was in town with my son and was on leave for thirty days. I asked her if we could come and stay with her while I was on leave and that I would pay her for our stay. She agreed and came and picked us up. I cared for her but I did not want her to try to live life through me because I felt like she was another force trying to control me and I was tired of trying to please people outside of myself. I shared with her my hardships and the actions of my son's father. She was more than willing to help me out and she did not go unrewarded for her actions. I was at peace that my son was in a safe, clean and healthy environment. That gave me the peace I needed until his father could come and get him. There was no problem with the father and son's relationship, just with me and father. I could not accept that any more for my life. The story does not end here but it does pause for the cause so I could gather myself and find me again.*

While visiting home I was reconnecting with people I had lost contact with. I made contact with my best friend and she met my son for the first time, and I was maturing and I also wanted my mother to meet her first grandchild. The visits went well and I saw how they were living. Not to judge, but I did not want to subject my child to my family's life style. I would have to provide for him in my absence, but could I be assured that his every need would be met. So I would not have a peaceful mind if I left my son with my family. Again, the visit went well but I needed assurance and I knew it was not the season for this. I could feel my mother's hurt, but I did not want my child to suffer. So I pushed past it and continued to work on restoring our relationship. This was a process for both of us. The healing was beginning with small steps on my part. Please don't get me wrong, I have a heart that is big and I love my mother, it's just that I had a problem with the choices she made but I would do and give her anything I had. While I was visiting I noticed she needed a new washing machine so I went out and purchased one for her. My vacation finally ended and I had to go to my new duty assignment at Fort Stewart, Georgia. My MOS 27E TOW and Dragon Missile Repair

It's Time You Rise Above, Now!

Specialist I perform maintenance repair. The company I work in was forward support unit. The unit supports all the infantry companies. My desire was to work main support, I was always with the infantry soldiers when they moved forward so did my unit. Please note there were not many women in my field and we supported the infantry, which were all men. So it was rare to see women on the front line. But that is where I was roughing it out, carrying my weapons, with a full ruck-sack weighing 30lbs. on my back and a protective mask on my hip, helmet on my head, and I was ready for war. Day in and day out for six months I carried this equipment with me everywhere I went. I was in Saudi Arabia in the desert on the front line, seeing war with my own eyes. Was I afraid? To be truthful, no I was not. My life left me feeling numb from my emotions, and I was a loner. I cut people off from my life and did little to communicate with my past and focus on the assignment before me.

It's Time You Rise Above, Now!

I believe God had dropped me a nugget to let me know he was still with me and that I was not alone. One day I received some mail, which was rare because no one wrote letters and I was astonished. By that time my son's father had retrieved him and they were making their way to Texas. I was not concerned about their safety or welfare. So I could face anything that was ahead of me. Well, my mail came and it was a piece of mail from my new credit union. They had gotten my name wrong but it had still found its way to me in the desert. It was addressed to Shalom Smalls and I found that to be uniquely strange but in my quiet time I believe God was sending a message to calm my spirit and the word was PEACE. I never corrected my name. My checkbook and bank card shows my name as Shalom. This was a prophetic message that came to assure me that all would be well. So I received assurance that I was not alone in my journey and that God had angels watching over me.

As the war was being won and because the 24th

It's Time You Rise Above, Now!

Infantry Division were the first ones in when the war started, they were the first to leave and we were preparing to return to the United States, however, I arrived to my unit late after they were already on ground so when they were pulling out I had to stay behind to finish getting all our equipment returned home. I was assigned to a work detail to clean all equipment to be shipped home. Everything had sand in it and we could not ship the equipment that way so there was around the clock cleaning, 24/7 packing, and traveling to get the equipment to the port to be cleaned and shipped for me. The war was still going on we had to maintain peace so other units and companies on the ground could perform their duties. I had to remain 6 months longer than my unit and was left behind. I did what was required of me, cleaning and washing big equipment vehicles, tents, nets, cots, trucks, generators, pot and pans. Nothing could be shipped without it being cleaned.

During this time I was growing in leadership. I

enjoyed taking charge of issues and seeing tasks being completed. I did not have problems giving orders and delegating assignments. I was an E4 in the Army but I always acted as if I was a sergeant major of the company. I was not afraid of any task. My favorite mantra during this time of my life was "Lets make it happen." Great joy came to me seeing the end result. So the only people who had problems with me taking charge without someone having to tell me to take charge was the ones who felt threatened. So as a female in a dominant male environment, I was not so easily liked. My mantra to those who had a problem with me was to go get a life. I did not care what they thought of me let's just get the job done. I could quickly spot the people who were trying to get over. I had never met so many lazy people in my life. Do the work that you are assigned to do; if not, move out of my way. Now the time came for me to return to the USA and I was more than ready. I was ready to see my son again. I was ready to get my son back in my life. Returning to Fort Stewart we were greeted by the entire community. Everyone was in place to welcome us back home and we marched in parade after parade and were given lots of down time.

We were given plenty of time to readjust to normal conditions to spend time with family and friends while waiting for all our equipment to return from the gulf. I was stationed in Hinesville, Georgia which is close to Savannah, Georgia right on the border of the South Carolina line and I was two and half hours from home. So I spent many weekends visiting my hometown of Charleston and other times I stayed on base. I did not have a vehicle at the time so I did things like hanging out with my girlfriends and shopping. I was never the partying type but I hung out every now and then. I had a cool circle of friends that were all mature adults and fun to be around. They partied and drank but I was never much of a drinker and I could not stand cigarette smoke. I tried to fit in with my friend but often I would drift off to myself and think about where life would take me and that it was time for me to put a plan in action to get my son.

So I never let my son's father know it was over between us. I invited him to come down for a visit so I could see them. I believe that was the worth mistake I ever made because he had not changed in any way. Still mean spirited and hateful, and I did not want my friends to see me upset about my life. But once I opened up and listened to myself, I knew I had to do something. Because he was now unemployed and I was the sole financial provider for my son, I asked him why not let me have our son, and that way it would free him up to find employment, and he agreed. He knew I wanted nothing more to do with him, they return to Texas. I needed to purchase a vehicle for myself, and find a place to live. I was on a mission to get my life in order. I remember all my friends had cars and all of them were red and remember one day I asked God for a car and I wanted it to be red. Four red cars parked in the parking lot. I remember praying and asking God for a red car for myself. I learned that God always answers my prayers just not to my timing, but he always came through for me. So the path that I took was I received a reliable vehicle in my price range. I had to be responsible and stay within my budget to run home. I was establishing credit for the first time. So I was satisfied with my newly used cream color 2000 Pontiac LE and it was my I was now able to go where I need to go without having to depend on any one that feeling was so liberating to me. Now I need to find a place to call home. I rented a two bedroom house in a nice neighborhood and the rent was five hundred dollars a month. There was another young lady looking to move off base and we talked and agreed to become roommates. This relationship was somewhat unhealthy. She did her thing and I did mine. We rarely spent much time together. We were on two different paths, but it did not put a strain on either one of us financially, so we were available to do this for a year. She then received orders for a new duty assignment and that was fine with me because I was at a place where I could maintain all the finances by myself and not struggle. During this time, I also managed to drive my vehicle up to Port Arthur, Texas by myself and find my way directly to my son's father's place. I was determined to leave with my son and if it meant I had to walk on egg shells and deal with mistreatment, that's the way the game was going to be played. I prayed before I got on the road, and I mapped out my distance and the time it would take to get there. I knew God presence was with me and that I was not alone on the assignment. I can truly say without a shadow of doubt there were angels with me. The time seemed to pass by and I never got sleepy. I drove nonstop from Georgia to Texas which was amazing to me. Now! Dealing with this man I had to stroke his ego. I let him think that we were in a relationship and we would eventually come together after he got himself right. But little did he know that I had plans to never look

It's Time You Rise Above, Now!

back and this unhealthy relationship of four years was coming to an end.

Chapter Two

My New Relationship

My new relationship was strong we connected. He taught some interesting facts about parenting a male child and how to potty-train him. This was a time when the power struggle between my son and I was being tested, and I was losing. I can hear my friend say, "Either you make him cry now or he will make you cry later." His saying never left my ear. I thought those words were harsh in my mind, but they were true and I had to deal with the matters at hand. I had to take control of this situation before it took control of me. SIDE BAR: What we don't master, it will master us or what I 'm not willing to control will control me. Our relationship grew. We were both young and I

It's Time You Rise Above, Now!

was a home body and he was the guy that hung out with his friends. The only problem that came in to play was that he loved me but liked other women. And when he got caught and I found out I had an STD, there was no way he could deny it.

By this time my name came up where I was allowed to move in to military housing. I would not have to pay rent and I would now live on base. This would cut down on my commute to and from work and I could move my son to the daycare on post. Our relationship did not end (an unhealthy relationship came in to play) but because there were such strong ties between us and he wanted us in his life, I began to make changes trying to do what was right. So we moved on and tried to establish a family atmosphere but he was not completely ready to give up his single life. He wanted me commit to him. This was not going to work but we made ago of it anyhow. Besides, my desire was for advancement in rank and now I was ready to do what it took to advance to Sergeant E5.

It's Time You Rise Above, Now!

And on the weekend I would go to church with my son and the services were rich and full of spirit for a military based church and I began to seek God for direction and I ask that He help me get promoted. I laid that at the altar and moved on. Meanwhile, God answered a prayer that I had prayed for a long time ago and I thought He knew what I needed instead of what I wanted. When I had proven that I was responsible to have what I desire that is when I was bless with a new shiny red Eclipse. It was a manual transmission. I had to teach myself how to drive this vehicle. I was not comfortable on an incline. My friend was driving my new vehicle more than I was, so I put a stop to that. It seemed like he could not find the time to be with me and I was seeing less and less of him so the hand writing was the wall. Then someone told me it was time for my re-enlist. I agreed to four more years and when I did I took an assignment to go to Korea. I remember asking God to let me travel and see the world and I was doing just that. I did get my promotion and I was now a sergeant in the

It's Time You Rise Above, Now!

United States Army. Life was moving along good and now I had to secure a place for my son for one year while I went to Korea. I not only came with a new assignment, so did my friend. We both were headed to Korea on a one year hardship mission where you could bring your family. Our relationship improved and I wanted more now from the relationship than I did before. He brought me a ring and put it on my finger and we went to Mississippi to visit his family for the holidays and though I was feeling some sense of security, I knew not to expect too much. This time in Korea it would do us some good. I met his people and they were nice. They welcomed me and my son. His mother said this was the first time he had brought someone home to visit his family. We were there for Christmas, and during our conversation I shared with them that I had to find a place for my son while I was in Korea. His mother said she would do it since she already had her grandson while her daughter was away in the military. So we agreed on some terms and that my son would be away from anyone who was connected to me. I saw their living conditions and I was comfortable and at peace. So my friend left for Korea before me, and I had five more months to wait. I began preparing for my transition, packing up all my belongings and visiting my folks in SC. I took my son to Mississippi and on I went to a new place I had never been before.

During my life I knew God was actively there and it was just that I was not actively in His, but I did not take for granted the day my first child was born. I recall my son's birth, and that he came on his due date. I can clearly remember when I was giving birth to him in the delivery room. There was a still small voice that spoke to me while I was on the table and I can recall the voice saying you will do this again in five years and then I heard no more. So the reason why I bring this up is because my son was four and I was on my way to Korea and my relationship from two and half years was there and something inside would not let me rest, because a desire was placed in my heart and I was not going to rest until it was fulfilled. We're now both in Korea and we were able to get together every weekend. My camp was small and isolated so he would come visit me often. I had my own room which meant privacy for us and we would watch movies and eat at the local café. We traveled to the nearby shopping area and sometimes we ventured off to a more exciting location like the city to go shopping. My spirit was in a state of unrest so I decided it was time for me to share with him what was bothering me. I wanted to share with him that I wanted to have a baby between us. I never questioned marriage, but I figured that would come later. I remember that he told me that I would have one year to give birth and he was to be the only man in my life. And my heart and love was real towards him. We made each other happy and I was free with him. I could be myself and share things with him. So it was no doubt in my mind that we were not going to be together. My camp was close to another small camp which was within walking distance. I would go there and work on pottery. I created many nice pieces and sometimes I would go to church at that location. And it was funny because the minister was Korean I could hardly understand this man. But I kept became drawn to the service. I remember one day walking to the cafeteria and I remember saying to myself that things were real calm in my life and that I needed to get prepared because a storm was about to come in my life. I really did not know the second half of the last line. But I did sense the peace in my life and I knew it was there longer than normal. So I needed to brace myself and get ready for what was about to come. What I did not know at the time. I believed things with my friend were moving in the right direction. I was weighing down on him, and I think he thought I was trying to trap him. I wanted him to give me my heart's desire. One thing I did not want to do was to deceive him. I was on the pill for years and I did want to stop without him agreeing. After my epiphany the week before then the weekend came again and as usual we had a good weekend but this weekend I asked if we could we go to church and dress up because in Korea you could take a suit out of a magazine and they would have it tailor made for you. Dressing up was the thing to do, you just had to have some where to wear it, so church is where we can go and we both sat and listened to the message. I did not take him to hear the Korean minister but we went to a service on base that we both could relate to. I listened to the word and the message spoke volumes. And I believe that day God was ready to share working on me. He was about to get my attention. During the week to come I did not hear from my friend and that was strange when the weekend came and went and I heard nothing from him. Oh, my God!!! Here I go again. What is going on? So here comes the question: what did I do wrong? Did I scare him? All kinds of thoughts ran through my head. The next week passed and still nothing. There is nothing worse than not knowing. I was stressed and through this I missed my cycle. I went to get a pregnancy test and it came back positive. I said to myself, how could this be? I was still taking my pill in my wired kind of way. I missed a day or two but would always get back on track. No big deal since the pills had been in my system for a long time. So, when did it happen? I got what I wanted I just did not know I would lose him in the process. In my spirit I could hear within myself saying "All that matters is the end result". And that was to give birth to a healthy child. Well, one day he called and I asked him what was going on and he said that he met someone from his past when he was stationed in Colorado. He said it was a female and my heart dropped. I realized he had changed and was no longer the same person. I did not know this new guy. It seemed like his heart was cold and disconnected and I had begun another unhealthy relationship because I wanted to hold on to him. I was pregnant and I had to walk this journey alone. And because my now ex decided not to re-enlist, he was due to leave Korea in one month. I had not seen this coming or the fact that he was cheating on me. One week I went down to his camp to shop and while I was on the bus I saw him and her. They were holding hands and were dress identically. I said to myself what the hell, we never did that. It was childish of me and I was hurt and jealous, but no way was I going to lose him. So I pressured him to be in his presence before he was to leave. I know it was hard for him because he was trying to juggle both of us and I knew it was just a thing between them and it would pass. I was willing to live this way and I still had five months of my tour and I was pregnant. What a place to be in. Since I had plenty of time on my hands to think and be alone I needed help and I needed God because I was beginning to come undone. So I continued to go to church. I was looking for comfort as well as direction. I was back listening to the Korean minister and this time I tuned in so well I understood his message. As he was ministering I remember the words being painted out in my mind. I saw myself in this chair and I was seated on the throne and it was time for me to surrender *and give God his rightful place in my life. No longer would I be seated there if God was going to rule my life and I was ready. I did not want to feel the pain I was feeling, walking in shame having another child out of wedlock. I had to know this was a part of God's plan to draw me to him and lean on him with every fiber of my being. I knew this child was a gift from God and the enemy was mad and yes the spirit was right when he said I would have another in five, my son and daughter are five years apart. I was in a vehicle with my commander and a driver and you would not believe it but we were in an accident. The vehicle was decked and no harm came to us. We were all shaken up and I knew that attack was launched for me. I was pregnant and I was supposed to lose the baby but an angel had a hedge around me. I could hear the voice in my head but nothing mattered but the end result. I stood strong in my conviction and I began to move on with my life. Then I received my next duty assignment and I was due to go to Fort Benning, Georgia. So six months pregnant and back on U.S. soil, I traveled to Mississippi to pick up my son and head to Georgia. I did not see my ex while I was there so I just moved on with my life but the soul ties were so strong and I would easily find the comfort I needed to move on with life. I was starting my process of truly being saved and living for Jesus and being a single parent was my focus. I received housing right away and I waited for my transportation to deliver my shipping. I had the stuff I packed when I was in Fort Stewart and the shipment from Korea coming. I had a three bedroom house, and I would fill every room. I asked one of my sisters if she would stay with me and she agreed to help me with my son, unpack my things, and be there for me. The enemy was really attacking me and I was going through so much warfare. I could not understand all that I was going through. My soul was under attack and the enemy did not want to let me go. I did not consider myself to be all out there, but the devil knew my future better than I did. So my Christ-like character was being developed and my*

It's Time You Rise Above, Now!

flesh still wanted the things of the world. My daughter was born premature. She came six weeks early. It happened one day after church when my sister was home with me. I was eating dinner and when I went to sit down I felt the baby was lodged in my rib cage. I was very uncomfortable, so I tried repositioning her. When I pushed down one time, my water broke. It was the strangest thing. I went to the military's hospital and because my daughter was premature I had to be transported to a hospital off base that could handle the baby properly. She came November 21st and I would have to leave her in the hospital for six weeks. I would go see my baby but the nurse would have already fed her and I could not hold her because of all the tubes. She was born with a rare skin disorder and I was dealing with so much. My heart was broken from my daughter's father not being in my life. In my heart I want to have another child. This is not something I really want to endure in this life time. I don't wish to raise kids that I can't afford. In the past years, there was a suppor system and I was alone and depressed all the time. Car issues, amongst other issues were difficult to handle. I believe Satan my adversary knew that someday I would be a force that would do more damage to his kingdom. One of my buddies from Korea was now stationed at Fort Benning, Georgia with me and he was a source of comfort in my life. His family relocated and my walk with my heavenly father was growing. I can remember leading his wife to Christ, going to church on base and seeing how the church was anointed to the tenth power. The women would pray in tongue and the choir would move me to tears. The Word was always building me up on the inside and comforting my soul. I was growing spiritually I develop a prayer life and my flesh begin to die and I was starting to hungry and thirst for things of God. I was mentally in a place where I was ready to be baptized to be dipped in the water so the enemy wanted toset a trap for me. He knew I was still in love with my ex and he wanted to come see his newborn daughter. But he had a hidden agenda *because he was operating in the flesh. I was not strong enough to refrain from lust yet. The sad part of the story is not even a month had gone by when I discovered I was pregnant again. Oh my God!!! How am I going to deal with this again? All by myself, no mate in my life, my second child still in the hospital after being born six weeks early, and I was pregnant again. I was so ashamed of myself and there was no way I was going to bring another kid in this world and not be able to afford to take care of it. I was not emotionally willing to deal with this. So I had to take a tough pill and I decided the best thing for me to do was to terminate the pregnancy. It was bad enough to have one child by him but two by him? I was not going to allow that to happen. So I did what was necessary at the time for me. I wanted to have my tubes tied as soon as I had the baby. But the doctor talked me out of it. Stating you're still young and that if something ever happened to one of your two children, you might regret it. But my heart was hardened and I did not want to ever terminate a pregnancy again. I was forced into this position and it was hard for me to forgive myself for my actions. But I truly prayed and asked God to forgive me and I had to move on for the sake of my kids that were here with me to be a steward over. I just believed that I had sent this child back to heaven for a later time. I still had hope that we could be a family and I did not need the drama of another child. I never shared this with him and he will never know it unless he reads this book. While he was visiting he said everything I wanted to hear. So we reconnected and he would visit and I would deal with withdrawing from the things of God. But I continued to press forward even though I was falling short with sins of fornication. If you have never been spanked by God you never have been spanked. When God give me a good chastening I learned quickly. I was learning a valuable lesson. The God that I served was a jealous God and He was not going to share me with another. So it was time for me to mature and to just grow up and begin making wise choices in life. I needed to change but I was still not strong within myself so I began praying for myself and asking God to strengthen me. I did not want him to see my motives as selfish because I wanted God and I wanted my male friend too. I knew God was not going to have it at all. I was starting to grow spiritually again because when my friend would come to visit, I would not see him the same way. I was beginning to notice his flaws now. Before, he could do no wrong in my eyes. Why did I settle for so little in life? It was because I was not ready to die in my flesh. But he was starting to lose power over me. I was telling him I could not do what we were doing if he did not want to marry me. I knew this was not going to work because he was not willing to commit and he did not want to let me go either.*

Chapter Three

A Healthy Relationship Matters

Life was going good for my son and me. I was managing my life and parenting my child and we were happy. I had a babysitter in place for him, and I worked from 6am to 5pm everyday and no weekend duty came up. Even if it did I would try to give it way. There was not much field duty for me most of the time when the infantry were out on the ranges so there were no accommodations for female so the male soldiers would have to support them. I was safe in garrison until our whole unit had to go to the field and stay thirty days straight, but the babysitter was there to assist me. So I went on with life minding my own business and one day the guy from the shop came in the shop and said

It's Time You Rise Above, Now!

that someone was inquiring about me, "who me?" That did spark my interest, who was inquiring about me? So while doing routine maintenance on the missile system on the Bradley fighting vehicle we would have to travel down to the motor pools where the infantry company kept the equipment I had developed and admired while doing my job. I was focused on my work and I did not have time for anyone, I stayed to myself. I was lonely and I wanted someone in my life but I was not going to make it happen on my own. I considered myself a lady and I carried myself that way so I was not going to go man hunting. I move forward with my responsibilities and one day a work order came in the shop for a missile system needed repair. My supervisor sent over a team to the company motor pool to repair the system, the team was out all day running diagnostic testing and troubleshooting the alarms but could not repair fault. The entire day was done and the team was still out and the technician in the office could not leave until the team in the field were complete with their work, so the supervisor had everyone go to the motor pool to assist with the issue. We replaced circuit cards after circuit cards and when nothing would work, it was I who saved the day. I suggested we replace another card they kept saying was not the problem and when they decided to listen to me and replace the card the alarm cleared. They were finally able to restore the missile launched to the down position. The guy did not want to hear from me and when it worked out they all had to bow before the queen. We were finally released for the day and I got a chance to see the guy that someone told me was watching me. Somehow fate would caused us to meet. He was bringing a work order to my shop for repairs, and we talked and exchanged numbers. We talked and I went out on a date with him. I told him about my son and we went on several more dates before we started to get serious. I was happy someone really liked me and my son. WOW!!!!!!!! I had finally met someone nice and not mean spirited. Okay, I can do this, but I never ended my last relationship officially. So time came and I got a surprise visit my ex, he had driven from Texas and wanted to see us. Well my ex was here but he did not know he was not my ex because I had moved on without confronting the issue. And now he was at my house and I'm telling him it's over but he refused to let me go without trying, so he wanted to give me the VOLVO he purchased when he left Germany. I did not want that car from him so he could and would use it to control me. No Thanks!!!!!   Then my current friend decides to show up for a visit and I go outside to meet him and tell him my son's father was here and what was going on. Well I did not want my ex to act crazy and threaten to take my son. I did not know how this was going to turn out because a part of me was afraid of him; he was evil in my eyes. So my current friend was ready to do anything to protect my son and me. He had no problem pulling out his gun and wanting to use it and I did not want anything foolish to happen. I sat in the car with him and we engaged in conversation and I assured him that he would leave in the morning and to just be calm. We sat and talked and laughed about our day. It was getting late and both of us had PE (physical exercise) in the morning, so he left and I went back in the house. My roommate was home so I knew there would not be any drama I could not handle. So as I walked back in the house he was standing at the door watching me out the window and I was wondering what was going to happen next. He sat me down and he just wanted to talk. He said he was going to leave in the morning and my son would stay with me. He said he was watching me talking to that guy and saw me smiling and laughing and that was something he had not seen me do in a long time. So, he was going give me my space and leave. That morning he kissed his son and left without any confrontation. Was God with me or what! I was closing on an unhealthy relationship.

Chapter Four

Letting Go Isn't Easy

As time moved on I was getting back in the swing of work and leading soldiers again. I was growing spiritually and I had a hunger for the things of God. My life was getting back into a sense of order. I was a working woman, mother of two kids, and seeking direction for my life. I remember listening to a radio broadcast where there was woman minister, Pastor Ann Hardman. She was preaching the word of God with such power, that I understood her teaching and what I felt lead me to visit her ministry. I enjoyed visiting her church and feasting off the word of God. I remember receiving the gift of the Holy Spirit with evidence of speaking in tongues and I was introduced to tithing at the age of twenty seven. I can remember having a conversation with God. I said "God I come to you but please don't ask me to preach" and we left that there because I was afraid and I was not ready to know my purpose. Often times my daughter's father would come visit and we would be in a happy environment. I can recall when I knew that God was impressing on my heart it was time to leave the military. I would walk away from military life as I knew it and enter civilian life. Completing eight years of active duty and I had no direction as to where I was to go or what type of work I would be doing. I literally stepped out on faith. I had some money saved, plus leave time I had saved up to cash in. I scheduled transportation to come and pack my belongings and store them for six months until I could get them out. I felt like the biblical character Abraham, leaving my familiar and comfort to sojourn to a place where I have never been before, yet God had the way paved for me. I knew for sure that I did not want to return to Charleston SC. No! That was not an option for me. The best way for me to love my family was from a distance. But God never told me the place I was to go, so I left the Army a single woman with two kids and no direction. So we went to Mississippi hoping to make a life with my daughter's father. Although he agreed that we could come, when I got there, he was singing a different tune. He was staying out at night and acting strangely, and he was distancing himself from me. I was staying at his mother's but I was lost and needed direction. One day his mother and I were having a conversation and I can remember her clearly saying her son was not doing the right thing by me. So I took her at her word and called my best friend since middle school. She had relocated to Atlanta, Georgia and she gave me and my children an open door to come and stay with her for six months until I could get myself together. It was time for me to get my life together and at the same time it was hard for me to let go. This became such a stronghold in my mind since I truly had wanted this relationship to work. This thing was consuming all my energy and I needed to get my focus. I needed to be actively looking for *employment, securing child care for my children, and finding a place of my own. I knew there was no turning back so I had to have many talks with myself and find order and balance for my life. The journey for direction began with what type of work could I do? My confidence level was shot and I was wearing that tag around my neck again which said "REJECTED". I thought very small of myself. My self-worth was down in the dumps, and I remember God speaking to me and saying you think I would allow you to learn a skill and not to fall back on it? So I began looking through the want ads for employment and I saw an ad with a temporary agency to work at Scientific-Atlanta. They needed assembly workers and electronic technicians. My view of myself was not having any faith in myself. I applied for the assembly worker's position and told myself I would work my way up. But God had another plan in mind for me. I completed my resume and went in for the interview and shared my experience with the interviewer and he said I'm going to make you a technician and I got the job. I had to take a test on electronics the following Monday, so I went out and purchased a book on basic electronics and electricity and I studied that entire weekend. I took the test and passed. So one thing is complete, I have a job. Next, I had to look for someone to watch my kids. My oldest was already in elementary school and my youngest needed a care provider. I managed to always find someone within my budget but not always to my liking. Some providers were right for the job and some I just tolerated, but we survived them all. During the time I visited my best friend's church, which was Baptist denomination, I was there in body but not in spirit; I needed to be fed on a personal level. So one day while out and about I met a woman who was on fire for God and she invited me to her church and I agreed to come. Center of Faith church was small right next to a larger church that was drawing large crowds of people. I can remember standing in the driveway saying to myself I should follow the crowd but my heart said* to stay true to my word. I went in the church it was welcoming and there was a female pastor. Pastor Green, she preached the word with strength, power and she taught the word. The service end and she came over and introduced her self to me. She was well dressed from head to toe. The following Sunday I was back at the church and at the end of the service Pastor Green came over once again an said hello to me, what stood out to me is that she remembered my name. I was hooked and I joined the small church and began to grow spiritually. Every time the door opened I was there with my children. It was like I was fighting for my life to change for the better. I worked in an environment of 80 % men and I was not willing to deal with any drama, especially a new relationship. I was running for my life and every time the church doors were open I was there gleaning as much knowledge I could handle, and the church became my life line. I wanted and needed direction and I also wanted to see amendment in my last relationship, but God put a *stop to that thought. While in service we had a guest speaker and he spoke to me directly. He I would be healed from my last relationship because God had someone else for me. He is not the one and that I would need to start dressing up and fixing myself up because God was going to send someone new to my life. Well I heard the word and it saddened me because I knew I had to let go of the past and from yet another unhealthy relationship of four years and I was also excited that someone new was going to enter my life.*

Have you ever had more than your share of unhealthy (toxic) relationships and dealt with the pain of an emotional roller coaster that would leave you thinking that you're the one with the problem? You're the one with no to little self esteem, and little or no moral values having to deal with issues that make you want to compromise your views and belief system. You're settling for less than the best that life has to offer. I did not want to get in yet another bad relationship. I wanted to get focused because I did not want to attract the wrong men to myself.

Sometime God will send something or someone in your life for you to get the lesson or lessons out of their experiences. My next journey would take me through the next 15 years of my life. In order to grow you have to go through something and in order for me to help you with healthy relationships. I had to be a willing participant to play the part to gain the knowledge I now know. Radio host Steve Harvey shared that his father used to say, " There's no lesson like a bought lesson". You would really have to pay a heavy price for the knowledge that comes with the experience. I've grown and matured enough to be grateful for every relationship in my life whether bad or good because they were the tools to help shape and mold me into the woman that I am today. I see nothing as a mistake alone but was an experience to teach me a valuable life lesson. The area where I was weak, God used the experience to help me grow and develop into a mature Christian where he would get the glory from my life. So I do not beat anyone up nor try to make anyone look bad. My intention is to show that unhealthy relationships can be turned into positive ones. I am a strong woman of prayer and faith, I stand firmly on the promises of God and in doing that, I know He will prosper me in every area of my life.

So that new man did enter into my life and he came with honest intentions to make me a honorable woman. We wanted a committed relationship. I had been a single mother and I was weathering the hardships of doing things alone, so I was relieved when I was asked by him if I would be his wife and I said yes. This was our first conversation. But marriage would not come until three years later. We both had some growing to do and some doors needed to be closed.

Chapter Five

My Torn Family

We ended our relationship several times until we could do it right. Family life was being born and we grew together in some areas and in other areas we never managed to see eye to eye. He would say that I was selfish and in my mindset I walked in independent and I believe that was a problem for our marriage. I am a leader by default and it was hard to follow when no one was leading. My spiritual walk was always an important element to me because it cost me greatly to get to where I am today. So when I got serious with God, He got serious with me. I want God's best for my family and I desire change, and no matter what other people do, I want to be true to *the things of God and I was ready to know my purpose in life.*

I can say there were times in my marriage that many of my experiences were unhealthy. And they required sacrifice on both people's parts and to be committed even when I was not being treated fairly. But the assignment before me was to minister to my family, to my mate and then my children. I know the value of having a happy marriage and I know that God ordains marriages and family, so I want to do everything in my relationship to make things work, and learning and giving Gods unconditional love towards my family. However, after giving everything I had in me, I sought God for direction in my marriage and I remained true to my relationship even though it was not an unhealthy relationship. My prayer to God, father please intervene and fix what is broken in my life. There were countless things in my marriage I experienced that I was not proud of and rightfully ashamed. Whenever substance abuse is in a home it brings many demonic forces along for the ride. Physical, emotional, verbal and domestic abuse, all invite their way into your home. I was losing the battle in my marriage but I was going to win the war for my own life and the lives of my children. Fifteen years is a long time to stay in an unhealthy relationship but again I learned to love my mate unconditionally so I serviced him with the love of Christ. This was not good for the family as a whole, because the environment was unhealthy and I believe giving a person chance to grow but if they're not willing to change for the sake of others, then at least for the sake of themselves. Then there was nothing I could do to help my mate any longer so I decided I wanted a better life. I decided that good was not enough if better was available for me. I had grown in faith and my self-worth meant everything to me because I was growing and I knew what I desired in life. I wanted what was God's best for me and my children. I decided to stop settling for less and I decided to be the change I wanted to see and that *meant me leaving behind a marriage of twelve years. I decided to say good-bye to yet another unhealthy relationship. I wanted my father's best for my life. Why not? I'm no less than the person sitting next to me, in fact I'm just as good. I can say this boldly because I know who I am, and whose I am. I can and will be bold in my Father.*

The bible states in the book of John that beloved I wish above all things that you may prosper and be in health, even as thy soul prospers.

We should not want anything less than God's best for our lives. When we settle for less, we not only cheat ourselves, we cheat God. We should want to prosper in all areas of our lives, health, relationships, finance, and our spiritual walk. All of the areas tie together when we form a relationship with God and want His best for ourselves. No more heartache, disappointment, or being beat down when we come into fellowship with God. The bible clearly tells us to seek the kingdom of God and His righteousness and all these things will be added to us. Well, what are these things we should be looking for? Good health, financial blessings and healthy relationships. So we sit back and wait for these things to drop out of the sky when achieving them must begin with ourselves.

I do not claim to be a guru on healthy relationships but I have had my share of unhealthy relationships to know the difference. My desire is to empower you with tools that would make you want only good and healthy relationships in your life. I want to encourage and inspire you to know that we do not have to settle for less than God's best when it comes to having good and healthy relationships. When God created mankind he desired that the relationship we share between one another be good. The English Dictionary defines health as a condition or state of something. Healthy is defined as enjoying health and vigor of body, mind, or spirit. So let's break down the definition, the first word that stands out is enjoy, enjoy is taking pleasure in. Taking pleasure in health which is a condition or state of being sound in body, mind, or spirit; (they are one which internally equal YOU) freedom from disease, disease when broken down means being in a state of disease caused by physical feelings of pain. I did not know so much could come out of defining what healthy relationships could mean. Once we can truly define a word and gain clarity and understanding from its meaning, we can begin to appreciate the word. So the English dictionary defines relationship as the state in which two or more people, group, and countries, talk to, behave toward and deal with each other.

Let's say the word Healthy Relationship three times now. Let's do an Affirmation/ Declaration say with me:

Father, you ordained all things and you said that

all things you made were good. Father, you spoke mankind into existence, to coexist with one another to form good and healthy relationships among ourselves. I take authority over all my relationships, and I promise to never give my power away. I will ask for guidance and direction from the God within me, to order my steps, and the words that I speak. I'm entitled to have healthy relationships in my life and I will not settle for less than God's best for my life. I give up good for great. Because when better is available then good is not enough. I am different and unique, and I know it. Therefore I dare to be me, I will not blend into the masses, I have the right to be who I am and live the life I want with healthy relationships.

I have dealt with more than my share of rejection; I have experienced physical, verbal and emotional abuse at its highest level and all at the hands of a series of unhealthy relationships. So I can identify the difference between what is healthy and what is not. All these obstacles in life have brought me the wisdom and the compassion to rise above the pains and failures to know that there is work to help restore people who are facing and dealing with some of the same issues. My pain of rejection has become a platform. It has given me a voice to help set others free. My suffering would not be in vain if I use my experience to empower anyone looking to change. So I chose to be a voice for healthy relationships. Hurting people hurt people, and in my process of healing myself I will help heal others to have healthy relationships in their own lives. My assignment is to teach you how to rise above in relationships with one another. We must break the cycle of being in unhealthy relationships. I encourage you to be the best you, you can be, honor God and yourself; do the right thing at all times and successful, healthy relationships will come to you and not be a minute late. Come on, you have it in you to do it. There is a winner in you.

Chapter Six

Don't Cover Up the Truth

Being True to Yourself and Self Awareness

SOCRATES: Know thyself

In order to have healthy relationships, we must start by being true to ourselves. We can fool everyone around us but at the end of the day and night, we need to be honest with ourselves. Life is not a game it's a journey and you hold the cards to what you want for your life. All power is within you.

The bible states in James 1:22 But be ye doers of the word, and not hearers only, deceiving your own selves. For if any be a hearer of the word and not a doer, he is unto a man beholding his natural face in a glass. We draw to ourselves who we are.

It's Time You Rise Above, Now!

If you're a liar, then a liar will come into your life. If you're a cheater, then you draw to yourself people who are cheaters that will even cheat you. If you're a cheap person, then you draw people who are cheap into your life. Again, you draw to you what you possess in character. The law of osmosis comes into operation when two or more people are involved, who will be the greater influencer around you. If you ever grasp this wisdom of life you will begin making major changes in your life. Remember, we're trying to achieve healthy relationships. Ask yourself the question. Would you want to be in a relationship with you? Would you want to be in your company? You stop and ponder the thought and say to yourself that is "Pretty Big." It's time to make some changes, but only you will know the truth.

Have you ever took a nice hot bath and when you were ready to get out you placed your feet on the floor and stepped to the mirror that was all steamed up and foggy? You began to clear a space so you could see your face and discovered you did not recognize the person in the mirror looking back at you. You wondered to yourself how long had this been going on? Then you clear off some more space to see the remaining parts of your body. Just to say to yourself who am I? Where did all this come from and how did I get this way? Is this my best and can I improve? Do I want to improve? Can I accept my own flaws? Your awareness of yourself has vanished and you have become numb concerning your true being. You sit down on the toilet and begin to have a reality check because you have lost your identity from the inside out and let's face it for some of us, outside in. Who was that person looking back at you? Did you know her or did you know him? Well I can tell you if you don't know who you are no one else will. It is important to know yourself and also important to know what you want in life. If you don't make decisions and choices for your life someone else will. An important key to healthy relationships starts with you. Self awareness allows you to take ownership *of your own actions. It puts all the focus on you and nothing or no one outside of you is responsible. You will never overcome unhealthy relationships if you're not willing to state that the problem starts with you. And if you're the problem, then you can become the solution. So no one can make choices for you. You make your own choices. That's how you can become the change you want to see. You cannot help others until you help yourselves.*

An important key is when we see something about ourselves that we are not willing to address as true issues in our own life. That's the beginning for change because until we become sick and tired o being sick and tired, then and only then can change take place. There is always room for self improvement, but no place to have a negative mindset of one's self. On life's journey we all will have to come to the awareness that we have to transform our mind. (Romans 12:2) "Do no conform any longer to the pattern of this world but be transformed by the renewing of your mind

It's Time You Rise Above, Now!

Then you will be able to test and approve what God's will is. His good pleasing and perfect will.

If I asked you to take an inventory of ten things you like about yourself, could you do it? Do you even like yourself? If you don't like yourself, nine times out of ten, you will tend not to like the people around you. Sounds like a good exercise to do. Let's stop and list 10 things that you like about yourself.

*1.*_____

*2.*_____

*3.*_____

*4.*_____

*5.*_____

*6.*_____

*7.*_____

*8.*_____

*9.*_____

*10.*_____

Here is an interesting self discovery: The assignment should have made you look deep down

It's Time You Rise Above, Now!

on the inside of yourself for the answers and you had to write them down. Some of you may have had a WOW moment. So, if this assignment has moved you, you can ask yourself other questions. The more questions you ask, the better your understanding to give a better insight of yourself. What do you not like about your life? The more questions you ask and answer them, the better off you will become. These answers form your core values. Core values are traits or qualities that you consider to be the driving force in what you believe and who you are and want to be going forward. Write your answers down on paper, in your tablet, and or laptop. Writing is the key to resonate your truth.

If you cannot list 10 things you like about yourself, it's time to take your journey to self discovery. Please do the exercise. You have to do this for yourself. I can inspire you, but you will have to motivate yourself. In order to be true to yourself you have to know yourself. What are your likes and dislikes, what makes you happy, what makes you sad, what makes you mad? What drives you, what do you value. Who puts a smile on your face? When you think about people or animals what does it do for you? When you care about the things that are meaningful to you so will others. Start noticing and being grateful for your own life and people will do the same. When you know your worth you will not accept anything and anything will not be able to come in your life. Be true to thy self. When we learn to respect and appreciate ourselves, others will tend to do the same. When you honor yourself, others will also.

The bible says that we are fearfully and wonderfully made. You're God's masterpiece and it so important that you see yourself this way. I'm still dealing with healthy relationships and it starts with you. You cannot love anyone outside yourself until you learn to love yourself. You will never find what you are looking for outside of yourself. No one can bring you happiness; happiness is an *inside job that begins with you. No one can rock your world, only you can rock your world. You have the power to be the change you want to see in others. Only when you're ready to address and confess your shortcomings, then you can truly overcome them.*

- *REJECTION: is the state of being rejected, it's being dropped, being a castaway. Being blocked with things such as walls that you cannot overcome. I had to learn to overcome feelings of rejection.*

I had to learn to discover who I am in God because for so long many people planted a plethora of negative seeds in my life. People putting me down to where my worth and value in myself was extremely low. God is the only one who called me and told me that I was His beloved child. God called me, He equipped me, He qualified me and He validated me. Because God is for me; He is more than the world against me.

It's Time You Rise Above, Now!

Have you ever saw a behavior in someone that just made you so mad that it vexed the very core of your being. I had this experience and I also had to learn from my lesson here. I was condemning other people's faults and shortcomings. I attracted those same behaviors to myself, and I began acting them out. But the truth is, the behavior was in me all along. This is why I had to live through some of the same experiences my mother dealt with in her life. I was condemning and I became her judge. In the bible Matthew 7:1-2 Judge not, and ye shall not be judged. For with what judgment ye judge, ye shall be judge: Luke 6:37 Judge not, and ye shall not be judged: condemn not, and ye shall not be condemned: forgive, and ye shall be forgiven: the lesson here is to know you attract what you are. Like begets like, birds of a feather flock together. So what attributes do you have? Again be true to yourself.

You must identify, appreciate, understand, and have the right knowledge of every good thing that

It's Time You Rise Above, Now!

is in you and all that belongs to you, because doing this will give you the confidence and self worth that you thought possible. There is no need to tear yourself down or be hard on yourself. It is up to you to see what you want to see. Choose to see the good in yourself and in others.

Chapter Seven

Overcoming Rejection & Rising Above

REJECTION: OVERCOMING REJECTION WHILE PURSUING PURPOSE

Confidence is another great asset you gain towards self awareness and self improvement. An important fact you should know is that your inner beauty is your greatest strength. Your outward beauty has value but it's only short lived. When the outward beauty does not match your inner beauty, it will speak volumes to those around you. Be the best you can be. One of my mentors shared that what people think about you is none of your business. And you are not other people's opinion.

It's Time You Rise Above, Now!

So it is not what people call you but it is what you answer to; it's what you call yourself that matters most.

Acceptance of Others

Newton's theory for every action there is an equal or greater reaction. As human being we are always looking for someone to complete us and to find our happiest in them and through them. When we do this, it becomes the making of unhealthy relationships. Why would we place so much responsibility on someone else outside of us, and never place the value on our self. Then when relationship fails we quickly want to point the blame at others. A simple life principle that has been taught through the beginning of time is to "do unto others as you would want them to do unto you." A key to healthy relationships is accepting people for who they are. Every one of us has unique qualities. Did you know that no two people in the entire world have the same identical finger prints? There were over 6.79 billion people walking the face of the earth in the year 2009. WOW that is amazing in my mind. God made us different for a reason, so that the world would have diversity. This way we can become strength to those who are weaker in some areas and they can be strength to you in areas where you are not strong. Allow others to be who they are and learn to respect them. People will disappoint us and fall short of our expectations but that's where you have to learn to place people in their proper roles.

Maya Angelou said it best: "When people show you who they are, believe them."

Christ was the only person that was perfect, all other individuals in this life will not be perfect. So we have to be able and willing to only work on perfecting ourselves. That way you will take responsibility for your own happiness and no one on the outside of you. You've heard the saying before and if you have not here it is: You cannot *change anyone but yourself. You cannot add to this and you cannot take anything from it; it just YOU!!*

It is so important that you know that everything begins and ends with God. So what am I talking about in this book? Your development of "Healthy Relationships" has to begin and end with God; bad ones and good ones. Red, yellow, black or white, we are all precious in God's sight. Mankind is supposed to always be evolving, you as an individual, you're growing and changing every single day of your life. Whether you know it, like it or not, you are changing. So you're changing no matter what, whether for good or not. So my challenge to you is why not change for the good. Start learning to love yourself. This is all a part of your journey in life. What will you gain from all your experience? Are you willing to learn and have a teachable mind? How many negative acts will it take for you to wake up consciously and want better for yourself? It all starts by learning to love yourself.

It's Time You Rise Above, Now!

An important fact to know is that your inner beauty is your greatest strength and you cannot love yourself before you love God. Remember, he created you for His glory. That's the foundation for all healthy relationships. When you love yourself, you will know how to love others.

Jesus said unto him, thy shalt love the Lord thy God with all thy heart, and with all thy soul, and with all thou mind. This is the first of the great commandments. And the second is like unto it, thou shalt love thy neighbor as thyself (Matthew 22:37-39).

Do not give your power away

Have you ever been in a situation where you saw yourself powerless? It's not a good feeling because at this point you are not in control. Someone or something has exerted their powers over you. It's not okay for someone to make decisions for you without your permission. Let me share a story with you. During the course of one of my unhealthy relationships my suitor took it upon himself to not tell me the truth. That he was married (unhappily) and we began our relationship. During the early stages of our relationship, he was always making it his business to find fault with me. He was living a lie and there was no peace in his heart because he knew he was not being honest with me. So to take the pressure off himself, he spent his energy finding faults and belittling me. He was acting out on me what was eating at him on the inside. The lesson I learned here is if people are accusing you of a fault they need to stop and look in the mirror, because they are the guilty one. Oh, had he been mature and honest from the jump, I would have chosen for myself if I wanted a relationship with him or not. He should have been honest in the beginning, had he came with the truth, it was my decision to choose how I wanted to handle this. But he took away my power the moment he lied to me. Another way to give your power away is blaming others outside of yourself. Remember, we have a plethora of responsibilities for our lives and at the end of the day, only you will be held accountable for your actions. A mature person would take ownership for their actions. When you help yourself you help others. You cannot help others until you can help yourself. That is why you must know who you are and what you will and will not except for your life. You must know your self-worth and value. And again, that is to know who you are. A little secret here is: self worth and value are grounded in the renewing of your mind, which should be the mindset of God.

My mindset is something I have had to work on every single day of my life and truth be told, until we stop looking for happiness outside of ourselves, and bring the journey of self awareness and self improvement, we will always be incomplete. Because everything you need is inside of you. I have to repeat again EVERYTHING YOU NEED IS ALREADY ON THE INSIDE OF YOU!! All the answers to your life are within you. One of my mentors would say, "go within or go without."

It's Time You Rise Above, Now!

When we learn that happiness is an inside job we would not be so easy to give the job away. Then no one can ever have power over your life. And if they do gain power it will be something short lived. Because you will remember your worth, it's important to stay in a place where you are in constant remembrance of value. By the time you know who you are, and what you will accept for your life, you will make valuable, conscious decisions that affect you and those around you. You will appreciate all aspects of who you are as an individual. From the inside out, remember all beauty comes from within. What we reflect on in the inside will radiate outwardly; drawing to you like minded people who think and act like you do.

If you are looking for good healthy relationship and you are the smartest person in your group, I been told that it's time to pick new healthy relationship. True self awareness always seeks to better oneself in all area of life such as relationships, health, and finance. So leave behind people that are not good for you; people who do not have your best interest at heart; people who tend to tear you down, to make themselves feel good. It's time to say good-bye to unhealthy relationships. There is nothing more exciting than being around people who see the best in you and who bring out the best in you and who love you. They should influence you to want the best for your life.

Famous quote: "Associate yourself with men of good quality. If you esteem your own reputation, it's better to be alone than be in bad company."
-George Washington

Attitude

"The only difference between a Good Day and a Bad day is your ATTITUDE!"
-Dennis S. Brown

On life's journey your attitude is everything. Attitude is a mental state of mind or position you take regarding life's issues and circumstances. This means it's not what you think but how you think it.

It's Time You Rise Above, Now!

Basically, you choose how you handle life's issues; a smart way is to focus your energy for a solution and not the problem. Life's journey will throw you a series of curves and it's not what happens to you but how you process it; how you choose to act towards the situation and people. Have a positive attitude in life. It's how you view things. Is the glass half full or half empty or do you view your glass running over? Out of attitude comes enjoyment of life and gratitude for all life's blessings. Out of attitude comes disappointment and anger at some of life curves. Out of our attitude comes the way we view every situation in life. It is so important to have a good and positive attitude no matter what the situation will be. Look at it not as a failure, but view it as an experience that was needed. We do not know how strong we are until pressure has been placed on us. I've learned that everything we experience in life will not be wasted and that God has plans to use it for our own good. There are no accidents in life. The universe does not make mistakes. Let's learn to

It's Time You Rise Above, Now!

make the best of a negative situation.

Great quote: *You can tell a lot about a person's character under three circumstances. How they act on a rainy day. How they act when they lose their luggage. How they act when you hand them a ball of tangled Christmas lights. -* **Mayo Angelou**

It's Time You Rise Above, Now!

Here is an insightful quote called "Paradoxical Commandments of Leadership."

People are illogical, unreasonable, and self-centered --love them anyway.

If you do good deeds, people will accuse you of selfish, ulterior motives-do good anyway.

If you're successful, you'll win false friends and true enemies—-succeed anyway.

The good you do today will perhaps be forgotten tomorrow - do good anyway.

Honesty and frankness make you vulnerable—-be honest and frank anyway.

The biggest man with the biggest ideas can be shot down by the smallest man with the smallest mind - think big anyway.

People favor underdogs but follow only hot dogs - fight for a few underdogs anyway.

It's Time You Rise Above, Now!

What you spend years building may be destroyed overnight—build anyway.

People really need help but may attack you if you help them—help them anyway.

Give the world the best that you have and you will get kicked in the teeth —give the world the best that you have anyway.

If better is possible, then good is not enough.

Forgiving others and yourself

Forgiving people who have done wrong to you is the key to your success for attracting healthy relationships. Forgiveness is the greatest gift we can give to ourselves and others. There is no way around it; when you set people free, you free yourself. You have to allow room for people to be who they are even if they fall short of your expectations. Unconditional love comes from God

It's Time You Rise Above, Now!

and we are to show this love for one another. Forgive so you can be forgiven. When you do not forgive the other person, you're not holding them in bondage, you actually block your own graces to be free. You manage the majority of your time and energy thinking about how you can get them back. But blaming others outside of yourself does not allow you to move forward. Being unforgiving is negative energy in your life and it will attract that same energy into all areas of your life. Someone will not easily forgive you. Let's look at your life for a minute. Can you say that you have done all the right things all time and that you never failed or disappointed and hurt others? I can go further by saying you even let yourself down once or twice in your life. But you learn from the experience you brush yourself off and you get back up. People will always have faults, everyone has a flaw or two and if you think you don't then you just missed it. Free yourself so you can learn to free others. The world will be a better place when you exercise forgiveness.

It's Time You Rise Above, Now!

Balancing Healthy Relationships

A mentor of mine once shared that life gives to the giver and takes from the taker. When choosing healthy relationships we will need to weed out people who come in your life to take away from you.

That same mentor also shared that what people think about you is none of your business, and you're not other people's opinion. So it's not what people call you, but it is what you answer to.

A person who aids the dependence of other people is called an enabler. When an enabler assists in shielding and protecting people, they remain weak and crippled in their state of mind. They hold the person hostage and they are unable to change. Their power is then taken from them. In order to have balanced, healthy relationships we must begin with having only good and healthy relationships. When relationships operate in the law of reciprocity, then everyone wins. Everyone wants to receive but not everyone wants to give. Relationships should be where all people involved do their part to give. Everyone may not be able to give at the same level but everyone can give. So if you have relationships where you're not giving and are not receiving, then it is just an unhealthy relationship. Then the day will come when you're going to get tired. (And that would be a good thing because you will be ready to make some changes) When we have balanced relationships we can also have a balanced life which makes for a better world for everyone.

Do not take on assignments that have nothing to do with you. To the enablers in the room please stop holding up other people's deliverance. You are in the way. How can people learn if you are always coming to their rescue? I can assure you we all know people that always needing to borrow money or asking for things beyond the lines of certain boundaries. The lesson when it comes to money is: don't give or loan out what you cannot afford to get back. Do not hold what you do or what you give to people as a weight over them as a form of control. Remember the saying hurting people hurt people. Set them free and use you charity to promote healthy relationships.

Everyone I know wants to be loved and everyone wants to be appreciated. No one I know likes to be hurt and have regrets; coulda, shoulda and woulda from a bad relationship. So let's start today by attracting healthy relationships to ourselves. What you are looking for in other people, they are looking for the same thing in you. So when you wake up and you look in the mirror, you better know the person looking back at you and if you don't know yourself, start your journey to self discovery. Do you consider yourself to be a light to attract light? Are you honest with yourself? Are you willing to address the hard questions in your life?

It's Time You Rise Above, Now!

In to each life some rain must fall, and as w[...] interact with others we may experience heart ache[...] heart break and heart failure. But there is still lif[...] after all the rejection, from others. The experienc[...] did not enter your life to destroy you but to hel[...] make you to be strong and courageous, to stand i[...] the mist of opposition of unhealthy to health[...] relationship knowing that the victory belongs t[...] you. One thing I know that you may find yoursel[...] alone sometime but God is away with you n[...] matter what come your way. Who ever come an[...] who ever leave remember God will never leav[...] you. I share my experience of my pain, in hope t[...] one day know that I not only help myself but I hel[...] you as well! When we form healthy relationships i[...] our lives, it becomes the making of a better you, [...] better family, better people, a better church, [...] better community and a much better world. An[...] that should be enough to make you want to smile.

Art Mortell, "How to Master the Inne[...] Game of Selling," vol. 10, no. 7.

It's Time You Rise Above, Now!

A Short Course in Human Relationships

- *The least important word: I*

- *The most important word: We*

- *The two most important words: Thank you.*

- *The three most important words: All is forgiven.*

- *The four most important words: What is your opinion?*

- *The five most important words: You did a good job.*

- *The six most important words: I want to understand you better.*

Shawn Johnson

It's Time You Rise Above, Now!

Shawn Johnson

Email: <u>*riseabovewithshawn@yahoo.com*</u>
<u>*www.riseabovewithshawn.com*</u>

It's Time You Rise Above, Now!

***************About the Author***************

Shawn Johnson was born in Charleston, South Carolina. She is a true essence of a virtuous woman who is motivated by spiritual excellence. She is a teacher to some and a motivator to others. Her passions include seeing broken people become whole individuals and empowering them to become more productive citizens in their community.

She is the mother of four amazing children and the joy of parenting has been personally one of her greatest accomplishments. She has served in the Armed Forces as a Sergeant of the United States Army for 10 years and is a Gulf War Veteran. She has over 20 years experience as an electronic technician, in the field of missile and telecommunications. She received her B.A. in Religion from Luther Rice Seminary, Lithonia, Georgia.

She has given countless hours of service to her community in her local church working with youth and young adults. She also volunteers with organizations such as: Girls INC, Steve and Marjorie Harvey mentoring foundation (Girls Rule the World), Power to Stomp out Prejudice, Sand Box for our Troops, as well as many more.

It's Time You Rise Above, Now!

She served on the committee for the Atlanta Women Foundation, an organization committed to promoting community awareness and involvement. Shawn has also been recently selected to become a member of Women of Distinction (WOD), a nonprofit group focused on community outreach. Shawn's passion for helping other achieve their full potential is what drives her to Rise Above life adversities.

Shawn Johnson

www.riseabovewithshawn.com

It's Time You Rise Above, Now!

Acknowledgment

I would truly love to share this joy and honor with those who have been in my corner throughout this journey in my life. To my children Kerry, AJ, Shalonda, and Angel who all came to earth to allow me to be your mother and to share the love of God with you all. To Michael, you were divinely sent in my life at the right time and place words alone can not express my thankful heart for your kindness, support toward me and sharing in my dream of having a healthy relationship. To my best friend, LaShelle, thanks for being with me through thick and thin. To my mother, you are truly an amazing woman of God. And to my sisters and brother, thank you for giving of yourselves. Thanks to all my friends for the part they played in helping me shape and mold myself into the strong woman of God that I have become.

Shawn Johnson

Rise Above

Every individual in life at some time have wonder when will my change come, Will my dreams ever come true? will I ever see success for my life.

when can I begin to dream again and did God really speak to my heart. Am I a winner in this game called life? It's a wonderful place to be in when you can questions life. Why because life has to answer you. But will you be listening for the answer because one thing I learn and I want you to get this its will never be a question of if... No NEVER, but just a matter of when.

So I say YES your change will come.

YES your dreams will come true.

YES there is success for your life.

YES God did speak to your heart.

And YES there is a winner in you.

It's Time You Rise Above, Now!

You shall rise above.

Shawn Johnson

CPSIA information can be obtained at www.ICGtesting.com
Printed in the USA
LVOW130420270213

321700LV00001B/2/P

9 780978 716264